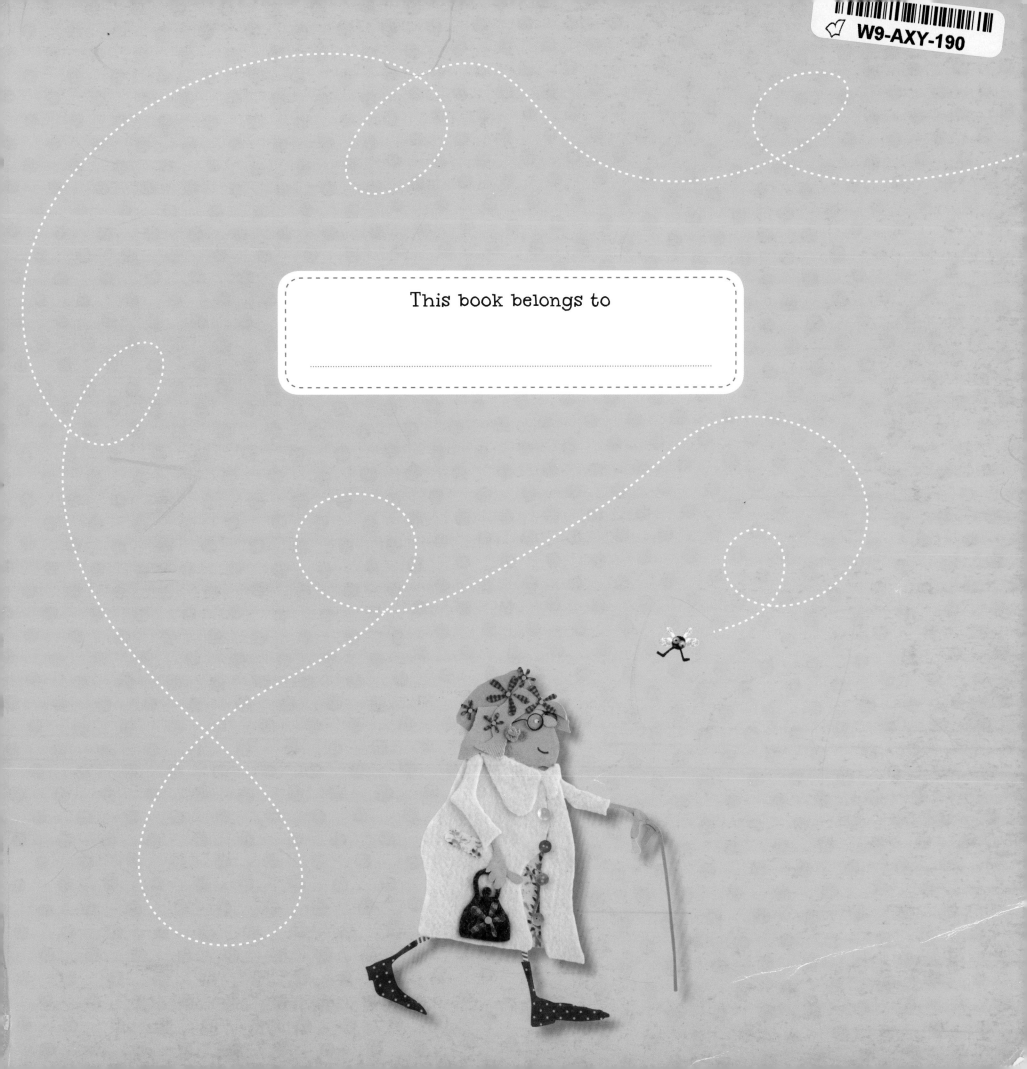

This book belongs to

....

Written and illustrated by Kate Toms.
Designed by Annie Simpson.

There was an old lady who swallowed a fly

Kate Toms

make
believe
ideas

There was an

old lady

who **swallowed** a fly.

Why, oh **why,**

did she

swallow

a **fly?**

Oh my, oh my!

Tra la la!

That little old lady was **walking** along, enjoying the sunshine and **singing** a song.

When **all of the sudden** a fly flew south . . . .

and ended up flying

right into her **mouth!**

That poor old lady – what a to-do!

Imagine if that happened

to **you!**

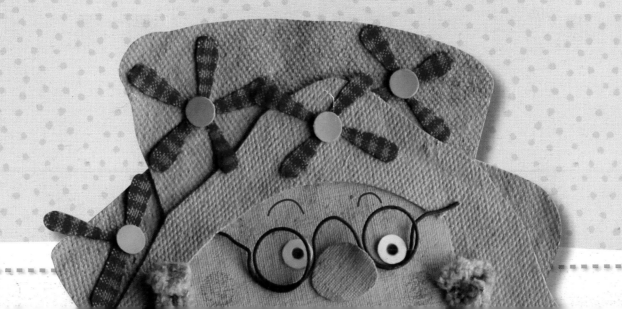

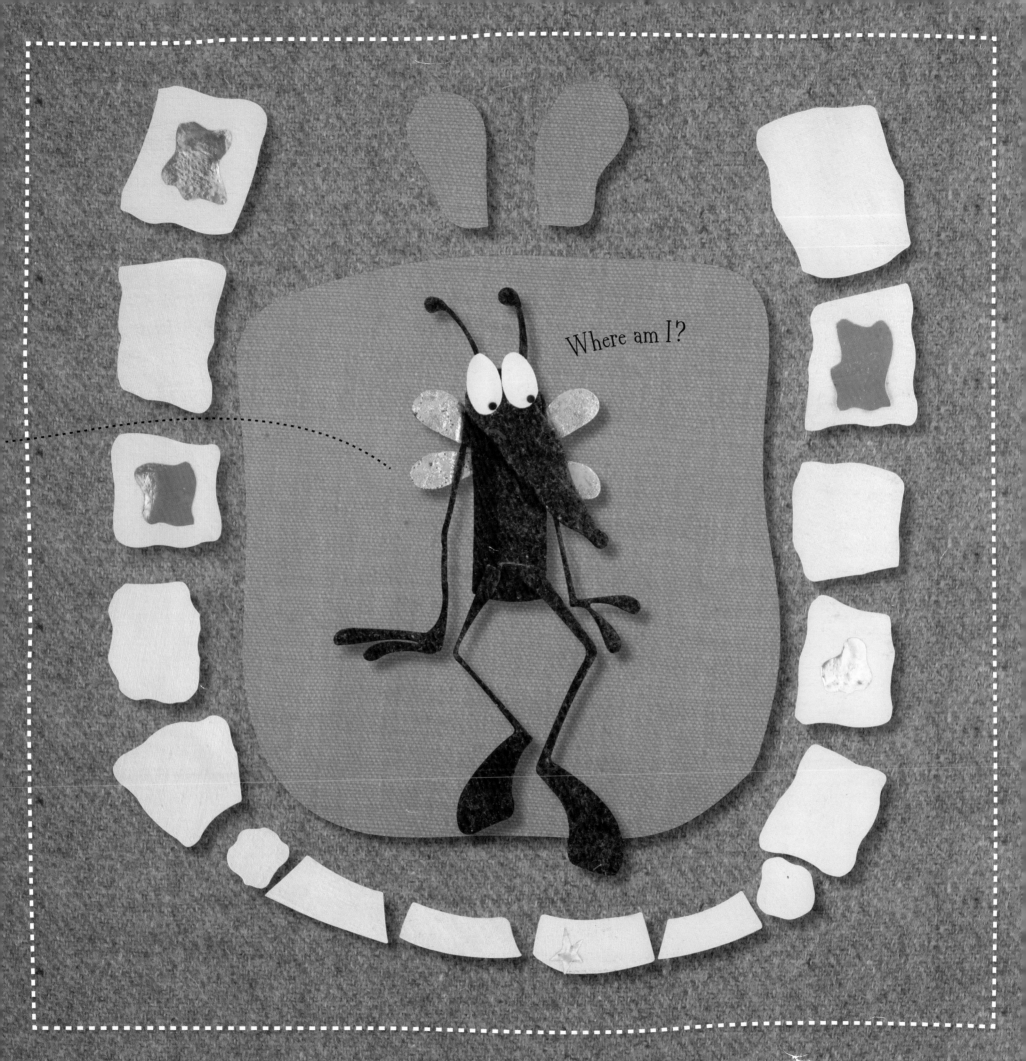

The fly now buzzes and
tickles her **tummy**
(she didn't think it tasted so yummy)!

But suddenly she has an **idea**

to make the naughty fly disappear:

to catch the fly she swallows

a spider –

so now she has them **both** inside her!

Oh my, oh my!

Down by the pond
she **spots** a **frog**,
sitting still on a speckled log.

Without even saying
"How do you do?"
she picks up the frog and
swallows
him too!

cRoAK!

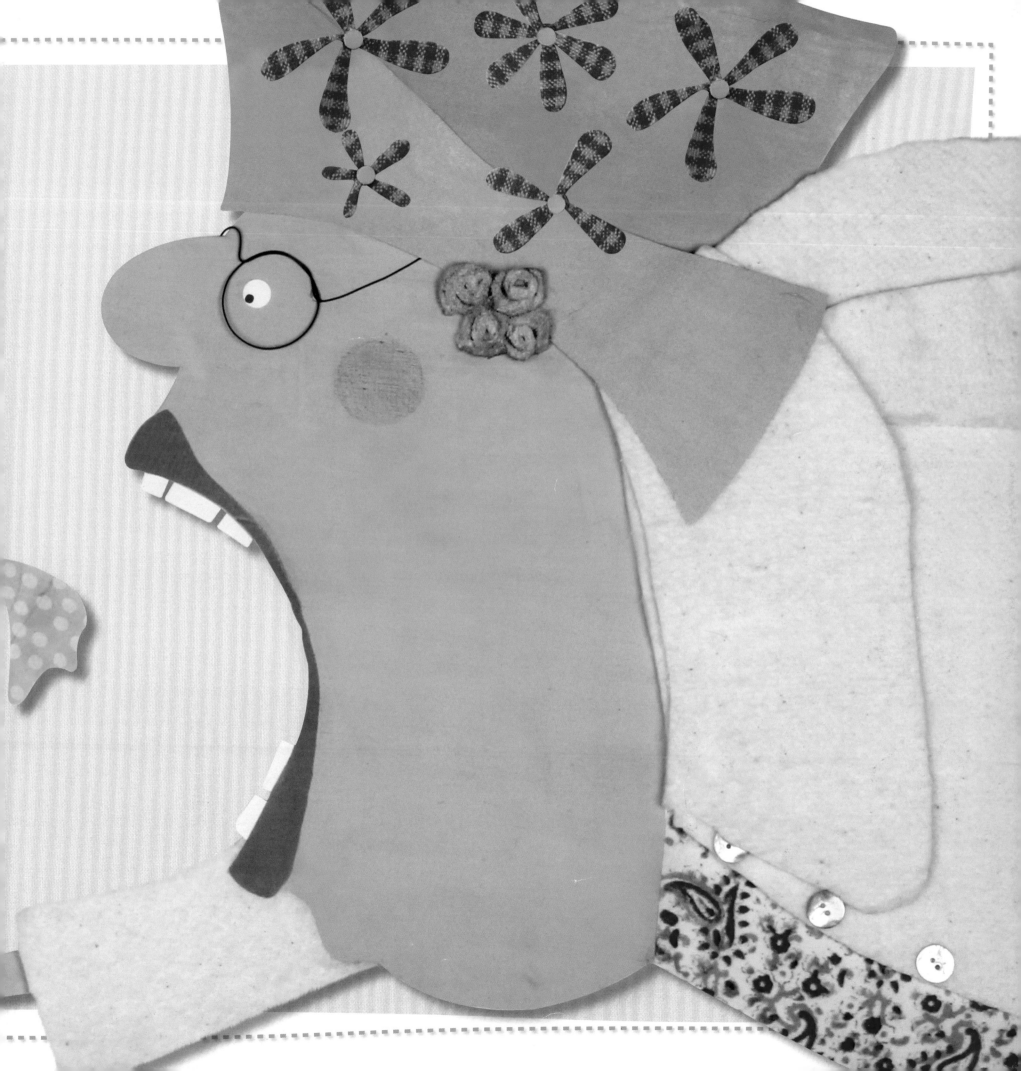

Feeling just a **little queasy**

(certainly not so bright and breezy),

she **spots** a heron on a nest —

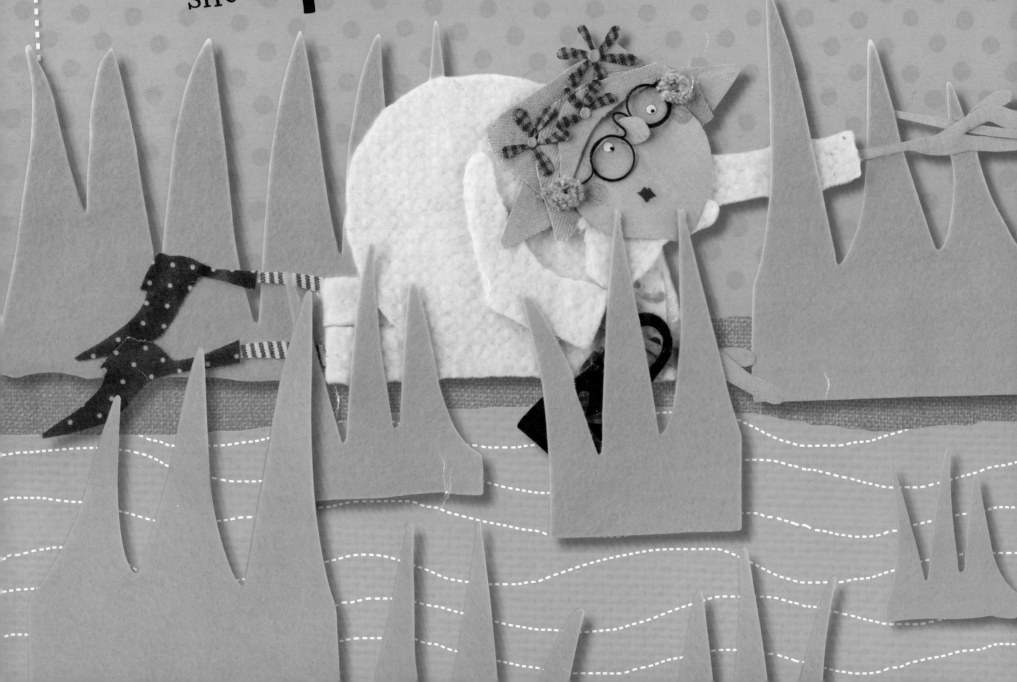

I wonder if you can **guess** the rest?

How could she **do** that?
We **don't know** how —
but you won't **believe**
what happens now . . .

Pretty Kitty

sits and **purrs**;

from behind her something **stirs.**

Before **poor puss**

has time

to flee . . .

she's washed down with a **cup** of **tea!**

Imagine **that,** to swallow a **cat!**

Oh my, oh my!

By this time it's **getting dark.**
Prince the **dog** plays
in the
park.

But poor old Prince
just does not see
the **old lady**
lurking by a big tree.

GULP!

Poor Prince . . . .

The old lady's **tummy** is about to **burst** – she wished she'd thought more **carefully** first.

She swallowed the **dog**
to catch the cat.

She swallowed the **cat**
to catch the bird.

She swallowed the **bird**
to catch the frog.
She swallowed the **frog**
to catch the spider.

She swallowed the **spider**
to catch the fly . . .

if **only** that fly had just **flown by.**

Oh my, oh my!